PARTY

To: _____

From: _____

Date: _____

My Birthday Book

Five Years of Birthday Memories

Written by
Catherine Hoesterey

Illustrated by
Mary Lake-Thompson

A Bulfinch Press Book/Little, Brown and Company   Boston • New York • Toronto • London

A heartfelt thanks to Denise Marcil

My Birthday Book is printed on acid-free paper to protect your photographs.

Text copyright © 1998 by Catherine Hoesterey
Illustrations copyright © 1998 by Mary Lake-Thompson

First Edition
Designed by Jean Wilcox
ISBN 0-8212-2399-2

Bulfinch Press is an imprint and trademark of Little, Brown and Company (Inc.)
Published simultaneously in Canada by Little, Brown & Company (Canada)
Limited

Printed in Singapore

For our children,

Sara and Abby Thompson,

Kyle, Daniel, and Nicole Hoesterey,

with happy memories of all the birthday

celebrations we have shared

A Birthday Book . . . Just for You

My Birthday Book is the perfect place to save the memories of your birthday celebrations. You'll find spots for keeping party invitations, pictures of birthday cakes, and photos of party fun. There is even a special pocket for saving birthday cards.

There are six pages to fill in for each year of birthday memories. Here's how these pages work:

About Me on My Birthday — Use these two pages to help yourself remember important things about the past year.

My Birthday Celebration — Use these two pages for writing about your special day.

Birthday Memories — Fill these two pages any way you like, with photographs, drawings, or souvenirs from a special outing.

My Birthday Book also includes a calendar section for writing down birthdays of friends and family members.

Have fun creating your birthday book. May it bring you many happy memories for years to come!

Contents

About Me on My _____ Birthday
(age)

The most important thing that happened to me during the past year _____

_____

_____

_____

_____

_____

_____

A picture of me

My favorite things this year

Favorite friend _____

Favorite book _____

Favorite food _____

Favorite movie _____

Things I like to do in my free time _____

_____

_____

_____

_____

_____

A new thing I learned to do this past year _____

_____

_____

_____

_____

_____

_____

An interesting thing that happened in the world recently _____

_____

_____

_____

_____

_____

My birthday wish _____

_____

_____

_____

_____

_____

_____

_____

My Birthday Celebration

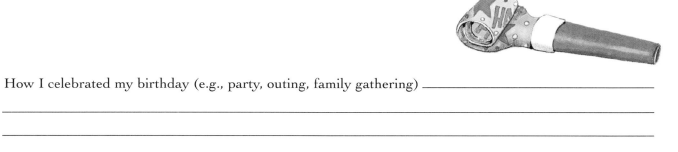

How I celebrated my birthday (e.g., party, outing, family gathering) _____

_____

_____

_____

_____

_____

[Place a party invitation or souvenir of your celebration here.]

Friends and family who celebrated with me _____

_____

_____

_____

_____

_____

_____

_____

A picture of my birthday cake

The best thing that happened on my birthday _____

_____

_____

_____

_____

_____

Presents I received _____

_____

_____

_____

_____

Birthday Memories

Fill these pages with photos, drawings, or souvenirs of your birthday.

# About Me on My _____ Birthday
_(age)

I am _____ years old.

Year _____

The most important thing that happened to me during the past year _____

_____

_____

_____

_____

_____

_____

A picture of me

My favorite things this year

Favorite friend _____

Favorite book _____

Favorite food _____

Favorite movie _____

Things I like to do in my free time _____
_____
_____
_____
_____

A new thing I learned to do this past year _____
_____
_____
_____
_____

An interesting thing that happened in the world recently _____
_____
_____
_____
_____

My birthday wish _____
_____
_____
_____
_____
_____
_____

My Birthday Celebration

How I celebrated my birthday (e.g., party, outing, family gathering) _____
_____
_____
_____
_____
_____

[Place a party invitation or souvenir of your celebration here.]

Friends and family who celebrated with me _____
_____
_____
_____
_____
_____
_____
_____

A picture of my birthday cake

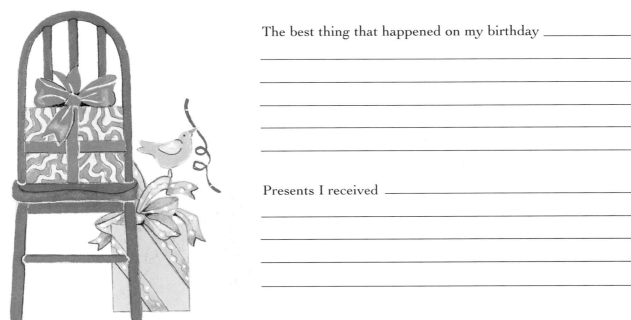

The best thing that happened on my birthday _____

_____

_____

_____

_____

_____

Presents I received _____

_____

_____

_____

_____

_____

Birthday Memories

Fill these pages with photos, drawings, or souvenirs of your birthday.

About Me on My _____ Birthday
(age)

I am _____ years old.

Year

The most important thing that happened to me during the past year _____

_____

_____

_____

_____

_____

_____

A picture of me

My favorite things this year

Favorite friend _____

Favorite book _____

Favorite food _____

Favorite movie _____

Things I like to do in my free time _____
_____
_____
_____
_____
_____

A new thing I learned to do this past year _____
_____
_____
_____
_____
_____

An interesting thing that happened in the world recently _____
_____
_____
_____
_____
_____

My birthday wish _____
_____
_____
_____
_____
_____
_____
_____

My Birthday Celebration

How I celebrated my birthday (e.g., party, outing, family gathering) _____

_____

_____

_____

_____

_____

[Place a party invitation or souvenir of your celebration here.]

Friends and family who celebrated with me _____

_____

_____

_____

_____

_____

_____

_____

A picture of my birthday cake

The best thing that happened on my birthday _____

_____

_____

_____

_____

_____

Presents I received _____

_____

_____

_____

_____

_____

Birthday Memories

Fill these pages with photos, drawings, or souvenirs of your birthday.

About Me on My _____ Birthday
(age)

Year
_____

I am
_____
years old.

The most important thing that happened to me during the past year _____

_____
_____
_____
_____
_____
_____

A picture of me

My favorite things this year

Favorite friend _____

Favorite book _____

Favorite food _____

Favorite movie _____

Things I like to do in my free time _____

_____

_____

_____

_____

_____

A new thing I learned to do this past year _____

_____

_____

_____

_____

_____

An interesting thing that happened in the world recently _____

_____

_____

_____

_____

My birthday wish _____

_____

_____

_____

_____

_____

_____

_____

My Birthday Celebration

How I celebrated my birthday (e.g., party, outing, family gathering) _____

_____

_____

_____

_____

_____

[Place a party invitation or souvenir of your celebration here.]

Friends and family who celebrated with me _____

_____

_____

_____

_____

_____

_____

A picture of my birthday cake

The best thing that happened on my birthday _____

_____

_____

_____

_____

_____

Presents I received _____

_____

_____

_____

_____

Birthday Memories

Fill these pages with photos, drawings, or souvenirs of your birthday.

# About Me on My _____ Birthday
_(age)

The most important thing that happened to me during the past year _____

_____

_____

_____

_____

_____

_____

A picture of me

My favorite things this year

Favorite friend   _____

Favorite book   _____

Favorite food   _____

Favorite movie   _____

Things I like to do in my free time _____

_____

_____

_____

_____

A new thing I learned to do this past year _____

_____

_____

_____

_____

_____

An interesting thing that happened in the world recently _____

_____

_____

_____

_____

My birthday wish _____

_____

_____

_____

_____

_____

_____

_____

My Birthday Celebration

How I celebrated my birthday (e.g., party, outing, family gathering) _____

_____

_____

_____

_____

_____

[Place a party invitation or souvenir of your celebration here.]

Friends and family who celebrated with me _____

_____

_____

_____

_____

_____

_____

_____

A picture of my birthday cake

The best thing that happened on my birthday _____
_____
_____
_____
_____
_____

Presents I received _____
_____
_____
_____
_____

Birthday Memories

Fill these pages with photos, drawings, or souvenirs of your birthday.

Birthday Traditions

What are some traditions your family has when it celebrates a birthday? We have a cake stand that spins around and plays the *Happy Birthday* song. It comes out for every birthday celebration. My parents had a musical cake stand when I was growing up, and now my family carries on the same tradition. Write down some of the special things your family does on birthdays.

_____

_____

_____

_____

_____

_____

_____

_____

_____

_____

_____

_____

_____

Birthdays to Remember

A calendar for writing down the birthdays of friends and family members.

January

1 _____	12 _____	23 _____
2 _____	13 _____	24 _____
3 _____	14 _____	25 _____
4 _____	15 _____	26 _____
5 _____	16 _____	27 _____
6 _____	17 _____	28 _____
7 _____	18 _____	29 _____
8 _____	19 _____	30 _____
9 _____	20 _____	31 _____
10 _____	21 _____	
11 _____	22 _____	

February

1 _____	11 _____	21 _____
2 _____	12 _____	22 _____
3 _____	13 _____	23 _____
4 _____	14 _____	24 _____
5 _____	15 _____	25 _____
6 _____	16 _____	26 _____
7 _____	17 _____	27 _____
8 _____	18 _____	28 _____
9 _____	19 _____	29 _____
10 _____	20 _____	

March

1 _____	12 _____	23 _____
2 _____	13 _____	24 _____
3 _____	14 _____	25 _____
4 _____	15 _____	26 _____
5 _____	16 _____	27 _____
6 _____	17 _____	28 _____
7 _____	18 _____	29 _____
8 _____	19 _____	30 _____
9 _____	20 _____	31 _____
10 _____	21 _____	
11 _____	22 _____	

April

1 _____	11 _____	21 _____
2 _____	12 _____	22 _____
3 _____	13 _____	23 _____
4 _____	14 _____	24 _____
5 _____	15 _____	25 _____
6 _____	16 _____	26 _____
7 _____	17 _____	27 _____
8 _____	18 _____	28 _____
9 _____	19 _____	29 _____
10 _____	20 _____	30 _____

May

1 _____	12 _____	23 _____
2 _____	13 _____	24 _____
3 _____	14 _____	25 _____
4 _____	15 _____	26 _____
5 _____	16 _____	27 _____
6 _____	17 _____	28 _____
7 _____	18 _____	29 _____
8 _____	19 _____	30 _____
9 _____	20 _____	31 _____
10 _____	21 _____	
11 _____	22 _____	

June

1 _____	11 _____	21 _____
2 _____	12 _____	22 _____
3 _____	13 _____	23 _____
4 _____	14 _____	24 _____
5 _____	15 _____	25 _____
6 _____	16 _____	26 _____
7 _____	17 _____	27 _____
8 _____	18 _____	28 _____
9 _____	19 _____	29 _____
10 _____	20 _____	30 _____

July

1 _____	12 _____	23 _____
2 _____	13 _____	24 _____
3 _____	14 _____	25 _____
4 _____	15 _____	26 _____
5 _____	16 _____	27 _____
6 _____	17 _____	28 _____
7 _____	18 _____	29 _____
8 _____	19 _____	30 _____
9 _____	20 _____	31 _____
10 _____	21 _____	
11 _____	22 _____	

August

1 _____	12 _____	23 _____
2 _____	13 _____	24 _____
3 _____	14 _____	25 _____
4 _____	15 _____	26 _____
5 _____	16 _____	27 _____
6 _____	17 _____	28 _____
7 _____	18 _____	29 _____
8 _____	19 _____	30 _____
9 _____	20 _____	31 _____
10 _____	21 _____	
11 _____	22 _____	

September

1 _____
2 _____
3 _____
4 _____
5 _____
6 _____
7 _____
8 _____
9 _____
10 _____

11 _____
12 _____
13 _____
14 _____
15 _____
16 _____
17 _____
18 _____
19 _____
20 _____

21 _____
22 _____
23 _____
24 _____
25 _____
26 _____
27 _____
28 _____
29 _____
30 _____

October

1 _____
2 _____
3 _____
4 _____
5 _____
6 _____
7 _____
8 _____
9 _____
10 _____
11 _____

12 _____
13 _____
14 _____
15 _____
16 _____
17 _____
18 _____
19 _____
20 _____
21 _____
22 _____

23 _____
24 _____
25 _____
26 _____
27 _____
28 _____
29 _____
30 _____
31 _____

November

1 _____
2 _____
3 _____
4 _____
5 _____
6 _____
7 _____
8 _____
9 _____
10 _____

11 _____
12 _____
13 _____
14 _____
15 _____
16 _____
17 _____
18 _____
19 _____
20 _____

21 _____
22 _____
23 _____
24 _____
25 _____
26 _____
27 _____
28 _____
29 _____
30 _____

December

1 _____
2 _____
3 _____
4 _____
5 _____
6 _____
7 _____
8 _____
9 _____
10 _____
11 _____

12 _____
13 _____
14 _____
15 _____
16 _____
17 _____
18 _____
19 _____
20 _____
21 _____
22 _____

23 _____
24 _____
25 _____
26 _____
27 _____
28 _____
29 _____
30 _____
31 _____

More Birthday Memories

Use these pages to record more birthday memories. You can attach photographs, make drawings, or write down more memories, wishes, or traditions.